Tony Mansfield was born in Dagenham in 1938 to a working-class family. His father was employed during the war, laying runways for the USAF and the RAF. It was normal during the war for children to be evacuated and moved to safe areas, but because his father was moving to different parts of England, he took Tony with him. Tony then attended junior schools in Wiltshire, Lancashire, Durham, as well as Dagenham. After his school years, Tony followed his father into the building trade and eventually into the property business. His interests include all sports, particularly golf and cricket. Tony is divorced but still friends with Gabrielle, and they have two grownup children and three grandchildren.

[handwritten signature]

This book is dedicated to my family and friends who have encouraged me, put me right, endured months of me not wanting to be disturbed and listening to me harping on and on about having writers' block.

Tony Mansfield

A Target for the Good

AUSTIN MACAULEY PUBLISHERS™

LONDON * CAMBRIDGE * NEW YORK * SHARJAH

Chapter 1

Mark Naylor was watching the 6 o'clock news on TV while he waited for Sue to get ready. Julia Simpson shuffled the papers in front of her and looked up at the camera. "Wayne Jones, the man being questioned in the case of the missing girl Anthea Gray, was charged today with her murder and will appear in court tomorrow morning." Mark tutted and thought that a man like him didn't deserve to live.

Sue came down, looking a million dollars in her new black dress and heels and said, "Come on, I'm ready. Turn that off, or we'll be late." It wasn't cold, even though it was the end of March, so she didn't bother with a coat, just a wrap over her shoulders. They were eating out tonight, the 30th March, at the posh Italian restaurant on the outskirts of town because it was their 19th wedding anniversary.

It was the first time Mark had been home for their anniversary. He'd been in the army since he was 18 and had done his 25 years, so he decided to quit and go home. He was comfortable with his army pension, and Sue had a decent job as manager in the HR department of the local chemical company, meaning that they weren't exactly wealthy, but they didn't have any financial worries. Their semi-detached house wasn't massive, but it was in a nice street, so they were both happy. As Mark was away a lot, they'd both agreed that there would be no kids.

Mark drove. He'd bought a decent little red Ford Fiesta when he left the army. When they arrived at the restaurant, they were shown to nice table. The place was only about 25% full and fairly quiet. After a glass of wine each, the waiter brought a menu and Mark chose the *Melone e Prosciutto* as his starter course. Sue decided to give the starter a miss, ordering a Caesar salad for her main course, with Mark settling for a steak.

They both looked up when the door opened and a well-dressed couple walked in to be greeted by name by the head waiter.

"Good evening, Mr White. Good to see you both again, sir." Mark didn't take too much notice when the couple were shown to a table, just in Mark's eye line. They both continued eating, but he couldn't help looking at the couple as he thought that the chap looked familiar.

After they'd finished their meal and were waiting for the coffee they'd ordered, Mark got up and walked over to the toilet. Washing his hands in front of the mirror, he noticed Mr White come in. He politely waited until White had finished peeing and was washing his hands before he approached him and said, "Sorry if you thought I was staring, but I couldn't help noticing you and was wondering where we'd met." White smiled and they started throwing dates and places at each other, and then it clicked. They had both played football for the same team when they were teenagers. They shook hands and had a laugh remembering names and incidents.

It turned out that Mr White, or Martin, lived on the edge of town, in the nice part, and had done very well with his haulage company. They agreed to meet up at the local Bull's Head pub the next night to continue reminiscing.

The Bull's Head was quite a nice pub, despite the awful curtains, and again the landlord knew Martin and shouted, "Hi Martin, you okay? How's Julie?"

Martin waved and smiled back, "Yeah, both fine, thanks." Looking round, he saw Mark at a table near the window and walked over and shook hands with him and sat down. They both had beers and exchanged pleasantries and spoke about their lives and where they were, what they'd done and agreed that they both felt the same way about current events, like the changing society and the lawlessness that seemed endemic, even in their own town. They also both agreed that the law was too soft on criminals and about the invasion of outsiders who were happy to live here but who didn't think it necessary to adhere to British law or contribute to the economy.

Mark thought that the law wasn't strong enough, and if successive governments were too weak to strengthen it, then maybe the public should shake them up somehow by showing their discontent. Martin agreed, but apart from complaining to his MP, he couldn't see what could be done. He was certainly past taking to the streets in demonstrations.

Mark thought for a moment and made the throw-away remark, "If I had a good enough rifle, I could shoot some of the bastards, and then the public wouldn't have to worry about them or support them anymore."

In fun, Martin asked where such a rifle could be obtained and if he had one, would Mark actually use it?

"The Czech Republic I would think, and yeah, I reckon I could do it," answered Mark.

"We go there quite often with loads back and forth," said Martin. They both laughed at the thought they shared but never stated.

After another couple of beers, Martin asked how easy it would be to buy a rifle and bring it back. Mark's guess was that a suitable gun would cost around £1,000 plus some ammo, and that it could be hidden in a lorry.

"Let's do it," said Martin.

"Whoa! Hang on," blurted Mark. "Importing firearms is bloody illegal, plus neither of us has a license. Anyway, it's bloody murder, so let's not get carried away."

They agreed that it was worth a bit further thought and swapped phone numbers and arranged to meet again in two nights' time.

Chapter 2

Now that he'd left the army, Mark was sometimes at a loss during the day. He thought that at 43 and retiring at such at an early age meant that he would still have plenty of energy and that there would be plenty of opportunities to devote his time to something worthwhile.

He'd done all the necessary redecorating around the house and tidied up the front and back gardens, so after about a year, he was spending too much time lounging around. Apart from football, he'd never been a great sportsman. He'd tried golf but found it too difficult. Tennis didn't really appeal to him, so he'd started reading the vacancies ads in the local paper without finding anything appealing.

One evening, Sue mentioned that a gym had opened on the other side of town and asked why he didn't give it a try.

Great idea!

Mark cycled over the next day and was quite impressed with what he saw. A nice-looking girl on the reception desk showed him round and told him what was available for him. There was even a good-sized pool. She also told him that they were offering a trial period of three months for £100, after which full membership was £50 per month.

Mark took out his debit card, filled out a form with a few of his details and paid her there and then. He then asked if it was okay for him to go along next day for a swim and a workout.

Yes, of course it was. He cycled back home and on the way thought that he'd probably go along two or three times per week. In fact, it killed two birds with one stone. (a) It would fill up quite a bit of his spare time each week and (b) it would keep him fit, fairly necessary now because he'd gained a few pounds since the army.

When he met Martin in the pub, he told him about the gym. Martin said that because his business life had occupied so much of his time, he'd neglected his fitness. Perhaps he should consider joining for say one or two evenings a week.

They both agreed that they would not only benefit from the exercise but by getting about locally.

Putting the world to rights came up again in conversation and Martin asked Mark if he'd given their previous conversation any thought.

Mark confirmed that he had, but it wasn't a decision that could be taken lightly. Martin agreed but thought that buying the equipment needed wasn't any commitment. He was prepared to finance the procurement of it, and he wasn't too concerned if it never got used. He suggested that as Mark was an expert, he could go along with one of his next lorries to the Czech Republic.

Two weeks later, Mark was a passenger in the cab of one of Martin's lorries bound for the Czech Republic. He had told Sue about his new friend Martin's business, and as he fancied a couple of days in a country that he'd never visited, an opportunity had arisen to see it, albeit in one of Martin's lorries. Sue realised that having had quite a hectic life in the army, Mark must be a bit bored at home, so she didn't have a problem with it.

It was a nice enough journey, good weather, and they passed through some very pleasant countryside. It was a two-day trip, so they stopped the night at a cheap hotel that John, the driver, knew about 50 miles north of Frankfurt. Although not stressed, both were ready for bed after their meal and a half litre of strong black German beer.

Mark had done his homework about weapons as far as he could, but this was all new to him. He knew the names of companies making rifles but hadn't a clue where to find the manufacturers. Google it! That's the answer. A few names came up, but most were miles away from Pilsen, where they were heading, except one, CZ Engineering, about 20 miles from the driver's destination.

Pilsen was quite a nice town. The old centre had been knocked about a bit in the war but rebuilt in the way prior to 1939 and looked really good. The industrial area was to the north of the town, as was motorway and train line, and there was plenty of activity. John had been many times before and he stopped at the hotel he normally used to let Mark out. A plumpish woman greeted him with a smile and showed him to a room overlooking the square. It wasn't exactly five-star but perfectly adequate, with a TV, a kettle and coffee and milk, which Mark made. He dropped his case and decided to have a look round. Next to the hotel was a bar and it wasn't difficult to order a beer and sit outside to soak up the surroundings.

A couple of hours later, John returned and they shared a few beers before having dinner. Both were tired and decided to get some sleep after.

Mark didn't think that one could walk in the front door of an arms manufacturer and walk out with a high-powered rifle without any questions being asked, but this was the Czech Republic, so nothing ventured, nothing gained.

He dressed in the morning and after having the normal continental breakfast of ham and cheese and a couple of coffees, he took a taxi to the arms factory. Someone there was found who spoke quite good English, and who took Mark into their very impressive showroom. Pistols, rifles, sub machineguns and shotguns were all laid out like a supermarket display.

Jakub, the well-dressed salesman, asked Mark exactly what he was after but not why he wanted it. There was one rifle that caught Mark's eye and Jakub took it down and handed it to Mark. It was beautifully weighted, and Mark balanced it professionally before lifting it up to his eye. It was very accurate to 2,000 metres, he was told, and could be bought without a telescopic sight if necessary.

Mark enquired the price and was asked first how he wanted to pay because dollars were preferred, $3,000 with a telescopic sight and 100 rounds, which was a bit more than he'd expected, but he was happy with the feel of it, and after a moment's thought, enquired if a silencer could be fitted. For another $800, Jakub confirmed that of course it could be and because technology had improved so much, a silencer didn't affect accuracy as much as it once did. Mark shook hands and told him that he'd be back in the morning with the cash.

That night after a dinner of goulash, which was really very good, Mark called Martin from his room to give him the news and was told that he'd try to arrange the cash in the morning and that he'd call back.

True to his word, about 11 the next morning, he called to tell him to go to the Ceskoslovenska Banka with his passport and ask for Jan Kova.

Mark jumped in a taxi and showed the driver a piece of paper with the bank's address he'd written on it. When they arrived, Jan greeted Martin like an old friend.

Amazing how they could all speak good English, thought Mark. He was taken in to Jan's office where he asked to see Mark's passport and to sign a couple of papers. Once that was done, he handed Mark an envelope containing $3,800 and £300 in Koruna-crowns. That was handy because Mark was having to be careful with spending. He'd bought a silver bracelet for Sue, which had cost a bit more than he'd bargained for, but he thought that as he'd told her that it was just a few days' trip away, it might be a little recompense.

There were plenty of taxis around outside, so he jumped into one and showed the driver the card that Jakub had given him. The driver nodded, slammed down the accelerator and they were there in no time. Mark was welcomed back and they went to Jakub's office where he passed over the money. After carefully counting it, Jakub handed over a very nice, shiny black bag with the company's name on it and containing the rifle. They shook hands and Mark left. He was amazed how easy it had been and wondered how many handguns were bought there and smuggled back home.

The trip back was uneventful, and they stayed in a hotel just north of Paris and then followed an easy drive up to

Calais. There was a small holdup outside Calais. Immigrants were blocking the road and trying to get in the back of lorries going to England. The French police were certainly not being too soft on them, and Mark laughingly mentioned to John that maybe our police should have the same attitude.

He was worried that when they reached Calais, the x-ray machine that searched lorries for anything suspicious would show up the rifle. But he needn't have worried; prior to leaving England, Martin had installed a lead-lined box behind the driver's seat into which the rifle and ammo were placed. He'd also given the driver £100 in cash to keep quiet. Mark still wasn't happy though, so he got down from the lorry and started chatting to the man watching the x-ray screen. He held his breath as the cab of the lorry containing the black box shape came up on the screen, but it was quickly passed. The lorry was given permission to proceed and a very relieved Mark got back into the cab.

Once back in Folkestone, it only took about two hours before Mark and Martin met in Martin's office.

Chapter 3

Weeks passed and news was announced that Wayne Jones had been released of the charge of the rape and murder of Anthea Gray on a technicality, and with a smirk on his face, had walked from court a free man. The police stated that no further enquiries would be made, and that there were no other suspects. The public in general were not at all happy. Comments were made by legal experts hired by the TV companies, and all the newspapers were calling for heads to roll.

A day or so later, the two Ms met in the pub, and the case was brought up in conversation. How about making him their first target? Mark hesitated but agreed to go along to where Jones lived to look at possibilities.

They didn't know Wayne Jones' address, of course, but it shouldn't be too difficult to find. They knew that he lived in Binley, a small town just outside Coventry, and after a couple of visits to the Dog and Partridge there, Mark had the exact address. He was a bit reluctant to always use his car, as there were so many CCTVs everywhere nowadays. Martin duly arranged for him to be dropped off by one of his lorries on its way to Coventry. Mark put his old bike into the back of the truck and when the lorry stopped briefly in Binley, he took it out and cycled the three or four miles to the field behind Wayne's house. He didn't mind cycling now and again. Along with his gym sessions, it helped with his fitness, which had suffered since leaving the army, and it was a nice sunny day anyway.

Fortunately, Jones' house backed onto the fields on which there was a small copse of trees, and which Mark thought would provide good cover. He'd made the trip several times and had told Sue that he was helping Martin with some heavy loads, so he'd be out and about for a few days. He watched the house for several days and decided that he wouldn't be too conspicuous, a few dog walkers had passed him, but they took no particular notice.

Mark told Martin all that he'd found out and thought that it wouldn't be too difficult to eliminate Jones. He was still very nervous about doing it, but after a few beers and some encouragement from Martin, he agreed, or at least he agreed to set himself up to do it once the opportunity arose.

The day came; it was quite warm, so nobody would take any notice of a man stretched out on the grass. The right opportunity arose when Wayne opened his back door and stepped outside for a smoke.

Before Mark had sat down in the field, he had placed the rifle under some leaves in the corpse. He had wanted to be a sniper in the army, but although an excellent shot, he couldn't always manage to get into the right position for the best advantage and had been passed over.

On seeing Jones leaning up against the back wall of the house, Mark lazily stood up, stretched, looked around and wandered over to the trees to uncover the rifle, which was already loaded. He was able to rest the barrel of the gun on a branch and, through the telescopic sight, was able to move the crossed hairs to Jones face. After a couple of minutes, Jones relaxed and took a drag on his cigarette, which was his last ever movement. Mark flicked up the safety catch, held his breath and gently squeezed the trigger. There was just a small thud and a kick from the rifle and Wayne collapsed with half his head blown away.

Mark picked up the spent cartridge, put the rifle in the bag, a different one to that which Jakub had given him, and disappeared over the field to the lane where he'd hidden his bike and pedalled into town, where he stopped for a coffee and waited for Martin's driver to call him.

Back at home that evening, Mark and Sue watched as the newsreader interviewed a police inspector giving brief details about the shooting and ended by saying, "If anyone had any information, please ring the number that appeared on the bottom of the screen."

Sue looked up from her book and remarked, "Serves him right. Everyone knew he did it, and it was probably only some other hooligan who he'd upset." Mark agreed.

Chapter 4

That same day, the telephone rang on D.I. Jack West's desk, and he took the call informing him of Wayne's demise and thought, *Thank Christ for that. I don't have to worry about continuing with that bastard. Someone has helped us out, good luck to him whoever it was.* Jack told the caller that he'd be there ASAP.

Jack was the DI who had nicked Wayne for the murder and was really pissed off that he hadn't got a conviction. He knew that Jones was guilty of the attack on that poor kid and hated having to tell her parents the terrible news. After the case, he had visited them again and promised them that he'd make sure that he'd watch Jones and make sure that he got him for the slightest infringement and would make his life a misery.

Jack didn't hurry to get to the crime scene. When he arrived, the officer at the front door acknowledged him and let him pass. The forensic guy, Dr Ivor Jackson, was already there and looked up when he saw Jack. "Not much to say, Jack, a pretty professional job, bullet from a rifle fired from some distance and half his head is missing."

"Hello Doc, any clues as to angles, etc.? It must have come from those fields at the back?" asked Jack.

"Nope, his face is a mess, Jack, but you can see where the bullet hit the wall, if that helps."

Jack carefully dug out what was left of the bullet and put it in a plastic bag. He'd give it to the munitions people and wait for their report.

As he drove back to the station, Jack knew that he'd have to write a report, but there wasn't any hurry. He'd make all the relevant enquiries, air brush a few details and put the case to bed.

Some hope! The deputy chief constable was on the phone, wanting to see Jack almost the minute he got back.

"Jack, we can't leave things there. We need to find out who shot Wayne Jones and why."

"Well sir, there were no clues, no CCTV round there of course, no witnesses, just a bullet that buried itself in the wall behind Wayne. There wasn't too much of that either, but the forensic squad should be able to identify it. His girlfriend swears that he had no enemies and managed the odd tear, but wasn't much help."

Jack agreed to keep looking, which satisfied the chief, who dismissed Jack and then picked up the top file of the 15 on his desk. The papers were full of it and all, but Guardian felt that justice had been done.

A few days later, the munitions team gave Jack a report on the bullet, which was Czech made and rarely seen in this country. After a few, half-hearted general enquiries, a man had been seen in the field behind the house, but no description was given and nothing unusual was noticed. Jack closed the file and put it in the pending tray.

Mark and Sue took up the invitation from Martin to come round for dinner that Saturday evening. Sue didn't know what to expect. She'd heard Mark describe Martin's business and how well he'd done, so she was just a little apprehensive. She needn't have worried though. Almost from the first moment they'd walked through the front door, Julie made her feel at home, and from then on, they got on like a house on fire. After dinner and a few too many glasses of Sancerre, and a very nice meal of *coq au van*, Julie took Sue for a tour of the house.

Being left alone, Mark and Martin smiled at each other and congratulated and toasted themselves and agreed to let things rest for a while.

Chapter 5

Abdul Karim had been imprisoned in his own home for far too long and at great expense to the British public, who had not only supplied him with, and covered the expenses of a house, but gave him disability benefit too. But he needed to get out and to preach his hatred of the infidels, in whose country he lived, but he knew that his presence on the streets could put his safety at risk.

He phoned his local imam to come round, and together they hatched a plan to get Abdul out and into the local mosque. Neither were aware that MI5 had been listening to every conversation in the house for over 12 months, either by tapping his phone or through bugs hidden in almost every room. He couldn't cough without it being heard. And translators gave MI5 the script of every word that was spoken.

After the army, a few of Mark's friends had found work in security firms, or as bodyguards, and Mark's pal Stewart King had been seconded into MI5 as a side kick and gofer to Max Roberts, a big wheel in MI5. The two friends spoke every couple of weeks or so, and sometimes things slipped out. One was that Stewart was currently watching Karim's activities.

Mark had seen Karim on TV, of course, complaining constantly that he couldn't even visit his mosque to pray, and that the time would come when white people would pay for their misdeeds. Mark and Martin had agreed that perhaps Karim could be their next target and it was handy because he wasn't too far away this time, and also they just might get a bit of information from Stewart.

Mark was a bit reluctant at first because he knew that MI5 were involved, and he didn't really want to chance coming up against them. They agreed, though, that it was worth keeping in touch with Stewart, just to see how closely MI5 were watching.

Stewart wasn't too forthcoming. After all, he was doing a job that he liked, and at the same time, earning a nice few bob and wasn't too stressed out.

Mark was cautious and didn't press him for info, but during one call, Stewart mentioned that he'd been given another MI5 suspect to watch because nothing seemed to be happening with Karim.

Mark perked up and took it on himself to drive to Karim's area, just to familiarise himself with the surroundings. The house was quite old and not very imposing, third in a row of eight houses, with a small front garden and a path from the pavement outside to the front door.

One day, he noticed a few photographers outside the mosque where Karim preached. He parked his Ford and slowly walked to the mosque and stood on the opposite side of the road.

He watched as a car pulled up and Karim, accompanied by two helpers, got out and amid flashes from the press cameras, hurriedly walked into the mosque.

Mark sauntered across the road and stood next to one of the photographers. "What's happening?" he asked.

"Nothing much," came the answer as the photographer got down from his steps. "I've just been sent here because there's nothing else going on today." Mark didn't hang around; he didn't want to be noticed.

A couple of days later, Mark met up with Martin to talk about Karim and how, if it were possible, they would manage to relieve the public's purse of Karim's expense. The rifle was out of the question, as was any close contact with Karim.

Then came an idea, during his army career, Mark had been given a two month's course on explosive devices. He wasn't too interested at the time, but some of it had sunk in.

He knew how to make a big bang without dynamite, just by using ordinary ingredients that could be bought almost everywhere. He also knew that various anti-terrorist departments had ways of detecting where, when and by whom, large quantities of bomb making material were being bought.

Over the next week or so, Mark started to collect the ingredients, not all from the same place or even from the same town. Eventually, he had enough stowed away in his garage but not enough to raise any queries from Sue.

He didn't have the knowledge to work out timing mechanisms, but he needed a remote to trigger an explosion, so he took a few visits to the library. He didn't dare try to Google it, and after a month of chatting with an electrician he knew, he had it figured.

A month later, Mark sat drinking a cappuccino in a coffee shop opposite Karim's house. He'd done this for several days but didn't make himself too obvious. This particular day, a car pulled up at the house and Karim's lieutenant, Mohammed, jumped out and hurried up the path to front door and rang the bell. Fitted to the door was of those new video doorbells, and Mark saw him lean into the bell and speak. After a moment or two, he stepped back and waited.

Karim appeared, looked round furtively, hesitated a moment, spoke a few words and turned to pull the door shut. He stepped out on to the front step, but before his foot touched the ground, the big green flowerpot next to the step exploded, and a hail of dirt, flowers, green stoneware, nails and ball bearings ripped into Abdul Karim about waist high. Body parts and blood together with some nails hit Mohammed, and he too collapsed. The windows and front doors in the adjacent houses were blown out.

Mark jumped up. "What the fuck was that?" he cried. Other customers were equally shocked, and a few cups of coffee and plates of cake hit the floor. Traffic stopped and a few pedestrians, including a woman pushing a pram, ran for cover. Within minutes, the police and ambulances arrived. The road was shut and taped off, and the police were speaking to anyone nearby.

They also came over to the café, but Mark and the other couple of customers couldn't tell them very much of just what they'd seen and heard.

Chapter 6

Stewart King's boss, Max Roberts, at MI5 was not too happy. With Karim gone, he'd lost a link in the chain of terrorists he was watching, which would be difficult to replace, and he wanted to know why. He was also aware that it had happened here, so the French would be critical and want answers.

What did Stewart King know? Nothing, apart from the obvious. Had he kept 24-hour surveillance? No, because he'd been told to split his time and watch others! Had he told anyone about Karim? No, of course not! Stewart had asked for the latest tapes from Karim's house, but unfortunately they hadn't produced anything telling. None of the neighbours in the adjacent seven houses had noticed anything out of place.

Stewart was worried. He had mentioned Karim to his pal Mark and wondered if there was a connection. Perhaps he'd mentioned it to somebody? There was no way he would mention Mark to his boss. (a) It wouldn't encourage the boss's confidence in him, and (b) it would get his pal Mark in an awful lot of trouble when he was probably quite innocent.

He didn't rush things and waited a few days until enough time had passed for another chat with Mark.

S: "Hi Mark. How's things?"

M: "Fine, thanks, Stewart. How's it with you?"

S: "Yeah okay, thanks. That is apart from the bit of a problem I had last week. You must have read what happened to that bloody preacher I was watching?"

M: "Oh yeah, he's up there enjoying his 40 virgins now, isn't he?"

S: "Yeah, and I'm getting it in the neck from the boss because I was supposed to be watching him. I remember speaking to you about him. I don't suppose you mentioned it to anyone, did you?"

M: "No, 'course not. Why would I? But I wouldn't think that there are too many people upset about it though, are there?"

S: "No, only my boss. He's upset because he's lost a link in the terrorist chain we've been watching, but hopefully it'll all blow over."

M: "Yeah, I'm sure it will."

They spoke for another five minutes or so, and then a relieved Mark let out a big sigh and gave Martin a call suggesting that they lie low for a while.

Chapter 7

Mark needed a rest, a holiday. He and Sue had enjoyed a fortnight in France a couple of years ago but he'd never been to Normandy to see the D. Day landing sites, so why not? Sue was owed a week's holiday and it wasn't difficult to arrange the channel train for their car. Four days later, they were in France, heading for Dieppe.

They'd landed in Calais fairly early, so it was an easy day's drive to Normandy. They found a nice hotel right by the harbour in Dieppe. The weather was great. The food was great, especially for Sue, who loved sea food. After dinner that first night, they sat at a table outside with a bottle of wine and chatted and watched the locals play a game of pétanque.

Next day, Mark took Sue to see Omaha beach, and she was very quiet as Mark described the action and the carnage. It was quite emotional for Sue, as she couldn't help thinking what it would have been like if Mark had been there in 1944.

Standing there, and imagining the scene, she gripped his arm a little firmer. They also visited the impressive American memorial, with the names of the thousands of Americans who had died fighting to help liberate Europe. Gold Beach was next, where the Brits landed. Seeing what was still left of the Mulberry Harbours, Mark marvelled at the ingenuity of them and wondered how on Earth they ever got those huge concrete structures over there. He also thought of the difference between those brave men that day and some of the scum walking free today.

Army life had not educated Mark in the culinary delights. There were many things that he hadn't tried, and one was Moule mariniere. He was in the right place, so why not? Sue tried not to laugh as Mark tried unsuccessfully to get a mussel out of the shell, until she couldn't stand it any longer. Leaning over, she picked up an empty shell, and using it like a pair of tweezers, she extracted the mussel out of its shell. "Oh, I see," said Mark and being a quick learner, he proceeded to polish off the other 30. He quite liked scooping up the wine at the bottom too.

After a very pleasant week, they drove back to Calais to catch their train home. They were quite early, so Mark drove around town to find a decent restaurant. He found a nice place just on the outskirts and as he stopped the car, a scruffy-looking, dark-skinned, bearded individual approached him and in stilted English asked if Mark could take him to England. Sue started to talk to him, but Mark shook his head and hurried her away, explaining that he was probably an immigrant.

In the restaurant, they discussed the incident, and both agreed that they felt sorry for the man, and if they were ever in the same situation, they would both probably resort to any means to better their lives. The manager came over and apologised for the situation, explaining in English, as best he could, that probably the man couldn't afford the amount that was being charged by the gangs for a rubber boat.

Once back home, and having a drink in the pub, Mark retold the story to Martin and it didn't take long for them to decide that their next victim should be the head of one of these gangs, but how to find them, and were any of them even in England?

"Stewart, I want you to have another word with him and see if he can remember anything important about that day. If he saw anybody new, or anything different."

"Yes sir, okay, will do."

Stewart wasn't too happy about this, but he didn't have much option but to do what was asked of him. He had Mo's address and, a couple of days later, paid him a visit.

Mohamed recognised Stewart and asked if he had any news or had any suspects.

"No." Stewart then asked if Mohamed had noticed anybody unfamiliar with him around the time of the explosion. "No," came the reply, "just the usual press photographers outside the mosque." Stewart then asked about the exploding pot itself. "Was it new, who looked after it? Was there anything odd about it?"

Apparently, the person who took care of the garden and plants had been used for years and was a regular Muslim worshiper at the mosque. The big green pot, was new and had been there for about a week. Stewart asked where it had been bought, so Mohamed picked up his phone and called the gardener, who told him that he'd bought it from that large garden centre in town, Jacksons. He'd bought that, and the shrub, and they'd planted it for him and delivered it.

Stewart thanked him and thought that he'd pay Jackson's a visit while he was in the area. It was a big garden centre, family run, with all the usual shrubs, trees and pots, plus some of those hot tubs which seemed to be getting popular.

Stewart sat down at a table in the café there. As he drank his coffee, he waited until an employee, dressed in company colours, came past.

"Excuse me," said Stewart, "can you help me please?"

"Certainly sir," came the polite answer. "What can I do for you?"

"I'd like to see the manager please."

"Yes of course, sir, maybe I can help?"

Stewart opened his wallet and showed the lady his very official-looking security card.

She didn't hesitate. "Ah, yes sir. I'll get him for you."

A few minutes later, the manager, Ian Jackson, the owner's son, came over and introduced himself, shook hands and sat down next to him. "How can I help?"

Stewart asked him if he remembered selling the large green pot to Abdul Karim's gardener.

"No, we sell hundreds of pots every week and I can't remember that one."

"What about the gardener I mentioned?"

"Yes, he comes here quite often. If you'll hang on a moment, I'll try to get some info."

Mr Jackson took out his phone and dialled a number. "Mike, come over to the café straight away, will you please?"

Sure enough, two minutes later, Mike came in, wearing his wellington boots, as he'd been watering some of the shrubs, and saw his boss sitting with someone.

"Mike, this gentleman is from the security services and is asking about a gardener we deal with, the one who looks after the grounds at the mosque. Do you remember him?"

"Yes, of course, he's a fairly regular customer," Mike answered.

Stewart then asked Mike if he remembered selling him the green pot.

"Yes, I do actually, quite expensive. He chose that and the shrub, so we planted it for him and delivered it. I heard about the explosion and always wondered if it was the pot we sold."

Stewart confirmed that it was indeed the same pot. Ian jokingly said, "It couldn't have been ours. We only sell non-explosive flowers."

Stewart asked when it was delivered. Ian disappeared for a couple of minutes and came back with an invoice. "Actually it was sent about a week before the explosion. All our transport was tied up, so we got Whites, the local haulier, to deliver it. We use them quite a lot because they've got a few vans for small loads."

Stewart thanked both of them and left.

Chapter 11

Gustavs Jansons sat down that evening to one of his favourite meals that his wife had cooked—Karpas. He'd caught it illegally on a nearby lake. He wasn't a member of that angling club, or indeed of any angling club, but he occasionally poached fish from there late at night when there was no one about and after he'd picked up the day's takings.

Not a sportsman by any means, Gustavs quite enjoyed fishing. He would sit there thinking about what he'd do when it was time to go back to Latvia. He'd build a big house and maybe invest in a local business. It was getting more and more difficult to avoid being caught smuggling in immigrants. He'd been told about police sniffing around the various 'massage parlours' that he owned. So far, he hadn't been questioned, but perhaps that wasn't too far away. Maybe he would have to think about selling the properties that he owned. He'd invested a lot of money into housing, which were all let out. Selling those would make it easier to slip away. The other problem was: would he be allowed to? He knew too much about the big bosses who ran the operation. They might not be too happy about him leaving. What he'd have to do was keep things running with a trusted accomplice and take a slice of the profits. Yes, that was the answer, and he had someone in mind.

First, he'd speak to Emils in France about his thoughts and try to convince him that his retirement wouldn't affect the operation. It might be worth keeping his flat and a grip on everything and coming back to London every month or so. That would allow him to visit his girlfriend that he had in one of his flats.

Chapter 12

Mark noticed that sometimes Gustavs varied his way home, nothing very peculiar about that. But one night, the Ferrari stopped by a lake and Gustavs got out of the car and peered over the fence. He went back to the car and took out a long bag, which he threw over the fence. He then walked about 10 yards to where the wooden fence was broken and slipped through the gap.

Mark looked on in interest. He watched Gustavs unzip the bag and take out a collapsible stool and a fishing rod. After about 10 minutes, Gustavs had fit the pieces of rod together, baited the hook from the contents of a jar and cast the line into the water.

Mark hated fishing; it was totally boring to someone who'd had a busy life, and he sat there waiting for something to happen but couldn't keep his eyes open. He was woken by a sharp bang on his window. Startled, Mark opened his eyes and saw a policeman outside. He opened the car door and the officer said, "Good evening sir, you okay?"

Mark quickly said, "Yes, I'm fine, thanks. I stopped to take a phone call and must have dropped off. Sorry, I'll be off now."

"Have you been drinking, sir?" asked the cop.

"No," answered Mark, "I haven't had a drink all day, except for a glass of orange and a few coffees."

"Well, in that case you won't mind taking a test then, sir."

Mark tried to argue, but the officer wouldn't have it and took out his testing kit. Mark got out of the car and hastily looked round and noticed that the Ferrari had gone. As the officer instructed him, he blew hard into the pipe. When he'd finished, the officer looked at the result, which showed all clear.

"Right sir, you're all clear. Sorry to have troubled you, but if I were you, I'd get home and get to bed." Mark thanked him, started the engine and drove home. On the way, the germ of an idea was starting to take place.

A couple of nights later, the two friends met in the pub. Mark told Martin about Gustavs' fishing expeditions and put up his idea. He knew where the fishing took place, and roughly the time, but not when. He guessed that the visits were about a week apart, so he'd give it a day or so more and try waiting by the lake.

Gustavs wasn't a particularly big man, but Mark, not a big man himself, was very fit and thought that he wouldn't have too much of a problem in a tussle with the Latvian. Martin was up for that but asked if Mark thought it was a good idea to get involved in a face-to-face confrontation with a victim. Mark told him that he'd been taught hand to hand fighting by the best, so he wasn't too worried about it.

Two nights later, Mark arrived at the lake at about 10 p.m. and squeezed through the fence. It was nice warm evening but a bit muddy underfoot. He hoped that Gustavs always fished from the same spot, so he hid himself in some adjacent bushes. After two hours, there wasn't any movement, so he thought it was too late now and extricated himself from the bushes. After waiting for a car to pass, he squeezed back through the fence. Sue wasn't too happy when he got home at 1 a.m. Mark made some lame excuse about the British Legion Club and climbed into bed. Better not do it two nights running, so if Sue asked, he'd have to have a good reason to go out.

Two nights later, he told Sue that he was meeting Martin and would probably be late.

After a few drinks at the Legion, he drove to the lake at about 10 p.m.

Although it was still a bit muddy, he didn't wear his wellington boots, as they would make a noise and could be a little clumsy in an affray.

He didn't have to wait long. He heard the throaty exhaust of the Ferrari arriving. Peering through the leaves, he could just see Gustavs get out and throw his bag over and duck down through the fence and go to his spot.

It took him about 10 minutes to get the stool out and fix up the rod, get it baited and cast into the lake. Mark waited another 15 minutes until Gustavs had made himself comfortable, and then being careful not to make a noise, he moved a few branches to one side and on hands and knees crept along the grass and stood up. He was a few feet from his victim when something made Gustavs look round. Startled, he began to stand up, but Martin said, "Hello, caught anything?"

Gustavs relaxed and that was his mistake. Mark gave him an uppercut with his right hand, not with his closed fist, but with the flat heel of his right hand as he'd been taught and the full force of his forearm. Gustavs went down on the stool, which collapsed under his weight. Mark dragged him to the water by one leg and slid him into it.

The cold water brought Gustavs round and he started to struggle. Mark had the advantage and put all his weight on Gustav's chest. His head went under the water and that's where Mark held it until the struggling and threshing around stopped.

Mark looked round. There was nothing out of the ordinary. There hadn't been much noise, but he waited a while and gave the body a shove with his foot. Gustavs floated face-down for a few feet and stopped.

Satisfied that the job was done, Mark went back to his car.

When he got home, he took off his dirty and wet clothes, put them in a black plastic bag and left them in the garage. After downing a glass of Scotland's finest to calm himself, he finally got into bed, trying not to disturb Sue.

Next morning was a Saturday and neither got up too early. Sue slipped on a dressing gown and left the bedroom. She came back with two cups of tea. Mark said thanks and sat up.

"So how was it last night?" asked Sue.

"Oh, you know how it goes," answered Mark. "Things got a bit out of hand with the drinks and before we knew it, it was bloody midnight."

"How was Martin?" she asked.

"Oh, he was okay eventually. He'd had a bit too much, so we called a taxi for him."

There was a moment's silence before Sue spoke again. "What's going on, Mark? I happened to phone Julie last night, and she told me that Martin was there watching TV."

Mark was stunned; he hadn't expected that. Sue wasn't in the habit of calling Julie, so the thought that she would contact her hadn't occurred to him.

"Sue, please don't worry about it. I should have told you, but I'm involved in something that I can't speak about."

"Mark, please don't lie to me. If it's a woman, I want to know. I understand that when men are away from home for a long time, some things happen, but you're not away now."

"Sue, don't be silly. There's no woman involved and I wouldn't be interested anyway. I'm very happy here and nothing is further from my mind. Actually, Martin is mixed up in this too, so can we leave it for the time being? But please believe me; we are not out chasing women."

Sue didn't seem satisfied but decided not to pursue the matter and disappeared into the bathroom for her shower. Mark contemplated joining her but thought better of it.

Chapter 13

As it was Saturday, Martin decided not to go into the office. There was nothing urgent, so he suggested to Julie that maybe a drive down to the south coast and find a decent hotel for the night might be nice, and she said okay. They'd been looking for a second home for some time, so a few hours around East Sussex might yield something. They had a lazy breakfast, and during a conversation, she mentioned that Sue had phoned her last night.

Shit, thought Martin. "Oh, that's nice. I like Sue. What have you two got to talk about?"

"Oh, just the normal women's stuff. She asked about you."

I'll bet she did, thought Martin. "Why did she ask about me?"

"Just about how you were really. I told her that you were a lazy sod and sitting in front of the TV watching the golf and drinking a glass of red." Julie went upstairs to pack a few things.

Martin sat thinking about things when the front doorbell rang. He got up and went to the front door. He could see a man's head through the glass and opened it to chap in a grey suit and open-neck shirt. "Mr White?" asked the stranger.

"Yes, can I help you?"

"My name is Stewart King, and I'm from security services. I'm looking for some information that I'm hoping you can help me with. Can I come in please?"

"Yes, of course. I'm not sure how I can help you, and we're off in a minute for the weekend, but I'll try."

They sat in the lounge and faced each other.

"Mr White, you may remember the incident a couple of months ago when a Muslim preacher was killed in an explosion at his house?"

"Yes, I do remember something about it."

"We understand that you deal with Jacksons, the garden centre people, and a few days before the explosion, Jacksons got you to make a delivery to that preacher's house."

"Well, we are a haulage company and we do have a couple of small vans to help out local firms with their deliveries. Jacksons have an account with us, but I wouldn't get involved with day-to-day running of that. Why the interest?"

"The delivery you made was of a large pot in which Jacksons had planted a shrub and was later identified as the murder weapon. So somewhere between the order being placed, and the delivery, somebody managed to load it with explosives."

"Oh shit, I hope you don't think that we had anything to do with it, do you?"

"We're looking at all the possibilities, sir. Can you give me the dates when you picked it up and when you delivered it?"

"Not off hand, I can't, no. I'd need to get out the files from the office."

"Perhaps you wouldn't mind doing that. Say Monday, sir, if that's okay? Here's my card and I'll be available Monday. I'm sorry to have bothered you, and thanks very much for your help."

Martin showed Stewart out and slumped back down in the armchair.

Got to phone Mark and let him know.

Julie came down. "You ready? Who was that?" she asked. Martin gave her a few details and shrugged it off.

"Look, there's something I have to do. Give me an hour and we'll be on our way."

"It's always the way when I'm looking forward to something," complained Julie, "so don't be long, or it won't be worth going."

Martin jumped in the jag and drove to the office. There was a bit of activity in the yard, but nobody was in the office. He took out his mobile and phoned Mark.

"Mark, we've got a problem. Your pal Stewart King came to the house this morning with questions about the murder of that bloody Muslim preacher. He wants details of our involvement in the delivery of the pot."

"Shit," came the reply.

"That's the guy who was in the army with me. He didn't connect you to me, did he?"

"No, he just wants dates really."

"Let me think about it and we'll have a meet. When does he want the info?"

"Monday."

"Okay, we've got a few days. Let's meet up Sunday in the pub."

"Okay, I'm going away for tonight, but I'll make sure I'm back in time, say 8 o'clock?"

Martin drove home and saw two going away bags in the hall. "Won't keep you a moment, just changing into something decent," he called.

"Well, hurry up then," came the irritated response.

Calm down, Martin, everything's going to be fine.

Ninety minutes later, they pulled up at a small hotel that had a room for them, and after dumping their bags, they found their way to the bar where they spent the next half hour downing a couple of glasses of wine before having lunch.

Chapter 14

Jack West hadn't had any excitement for ages. He browsed through some of the things that were happening in other manors and came across one that looked interesting. Investigations were going on about a body found in a lake by some fishermen. He'd been identified as an Eastern European and owner of a red Ferrari found in the street.

Named Gustavs Jansons apparently.

What's an Eastern European doing with a £250k motor? thought Jack. The name rang a bell with him. He phoned James J and told him to get any info he could on the name. Within 10 minutes, James came back to say that he thought the same man was associated with a massage parlour in Jack's manor.

Jack looked to see who was in charge of the case, and it happened to be D.I. Fred Wade, an old pal of his. Jack called him and Fred answered.

"What you doing nicking all my cases, you old git?" asked Jack.

Fred recognised the voice straight way. "You can have all my cases, you old sod. All I want is to get to my flat in Benidorm and never see any of these evil bastards again. What's up?"

Jack asked about Gustavs.

"Funny ole business," said Fred. "He was found face-down in the lake by a couple of the club fishermen. He wasn't a member, so obviously trying to poach a carp or two, out of hours. These Latvians like the occasional carp for dinner apparently, can't see it myself."

"Murder, you think?" asked Jack.

"Yeah, I think so. He ran a few massage parlours, that sort of thing, and rumour has it that he may have been tied up with people smuggling because a lot of his girls were foreign and afraid to talk. Unfortunately, security services are in on the act now, so I've had to take a back seat."

"Good to talk to you, Fred. The guy had a parlour down here too, that's why I was interested. Let me know if it goes any further please?"

"Yeah, will do, Jack. Take care."

Jack picked up the top file on the desk; it was the Wayne Jones murder. "James, in here please." James came in and sat down.

"We any further with this?" he asked, showing James the file.

"I sent the CCTV tapes to the face recognition department, sir, but I didn't hear anything."

"Give 'em a call and see if they've got anything."

James did as he was told and called them and was informed that they had looked at it at the time and couldn't find anything, but funnily enough, new technology had just emerged that only 50% of a face needed to be seen to be able to prove an identity, so they'd take look at it again. James reported this back to Jack, who asked to be kept in touch.

Chapter 15

At 8 p.m. on Sunday evening, Mark walked into the pub and found Martin already there.

A very nervous conversation took place.

"So what did Stewart ask?"

"He wants to know when we picked up the pot and when we delivered it."

"He'll want to know why there was a two-day delay between collection and delivery."

"I think I can cover those two days. I'll tell him that we had a driver problem and couldn't get a replacement for a couple of days."

"Let's hope he believes you. He mustn't know any connection between us. That'll really catch us."

"I'll let you know his reaction, Mark."

After lunch on Monday, Martin called Stewart King.

"Oh hello, Mr King. Martin White here. I've got those delivery dates for you."

"Oh great, let me get a pen… Okay, shoot."

"We collected the item from Jacksons on the 23rd June and delivered it on the 25th."

"Any reason for the two-day gap?"

"I'm told that we had a driver problem and it took two days to get a replacement."

"Oh, okay, that all sounds pretty reasonable. Where was the item kept during those two days?"

"I never asked, but I guess that as it would be pretty heavy, it stayed on the van."

"Okay, that's fine. Thanks very much for your help, Mr White. If I need any more, I'll get back to you… Bye."

A relieved Martin put the phone down and asked Joan, his secretary, to get him a cup of coffee. Later that day, he called Mark and told him what had happened. "Thank God," was Mark's reply.

Max Roberts called Stewart. "How's the investigation into the preacher's murder going, Stewart?"

"Well sir, nothing startling has shown up yet, but there are a few more questions to be asked."

"I need you to hurry up. Another problem has landed on my desk. You remember our enquiries into the people smuggling gangs?"

"Yes sir."

"One of the suspects, Gustavs Jansons, was found drowned and it doesn't look like an accident. We'll need to look into it."

"Okay sir, give me some details please, and I'll get on to it."

"I'll email you the location and some names right away."

They came through almost immediately and Stewart was pleased that the location wasn't too far away.

There was something not quite right about Martin White's story; he needed to think about it. He had looked to see what the service had on file about him. Nothing remarkable. No criminal activities, a few traffic fines, a few problems with his lorries but nothing serious. Perhaps a visit to a few local places might throw some light on how he was accepted in the area. Best place to start was always the local pub.

Chapter 16

The Bull's Head was a nice pub, with obviously a better clientele than some others. Stewart ordered a pint of IPA and sat on a stool at the end of the counter. It was a fairly quiet night and the barman was chatty. "You're lucky old Gerry won't be in tonight, sir. You're on his stool."

"Oh dear, I'll move if he shows up," said Stewart.

"I was having a chat with a chap who lives near here the other day and as I was passing, it looked a nice pub, so I thought I'd stop by."

"Every new customer is welcome. Who were you visiting?"

"I'm trying to find an answer to a problem we've got and thought Mr Martin White could help me."

"Oh yes, Martin. Nice chap. I'm sure he'd help you if he could. He's often here with his pal, an ex-army chap."

A bell rang in his head, ex-army type, Christ, he hoped not.

Finishing his pint, he said g'bye to the bar man and left. He didn't go far. He sat in his car and called Mark.

"Hi Mark, Stewart here. How's things?"

"Oh, hello Stewart. I'm fine, thanks. How're you?"

"Yep, I'm okay. Actually I'm not too far away from you, so thought I might pop in and have a chat?"

"Actually I'm a bit tied up tonight, Stewart. Perhaps another time, eh?"

"Mark, I think it might be in your best interest if I could pop in now." Mark recognised the tone of voice.

"Oh okay, do you know where I am?"

"No, I wasn't expecting to get in touch really, so what's the address?"

Mark gave him the address and after realising that Stewart wasn't too far away, he prepared himself mentally.

Fifteen minutes later, the doorbell rang, and Mark opened it to Stewart. They went into the lounge where Sue was watching TV. "Sue, this is Stewart, we were in the same regiment."

"Oh hello, Stewart, Mark's mentioned you. How are you?"

Several pleasantries were exchanged and Sue disappeared to get them a cup of tea. Mark followed her. "Sue, Stewart is one of the reasons I've been disappearing lately. He's here to catch up, so it's perhaps better if you leave us for a little while please."

Sue looked quizzically at him but agreed that she did have a book to finish.

When the two men had their tea, Stewart began.

"Mark, I think you might know why I'm here. I gave you some info that I shouldn't have done. Your friend Martin White delivered the pot which exploded and you're *au fait* with explosives. So I'm thinking…connection?"

"Christ! Stewart, are you suggesting that we were involved in the killing?"

"It all adds up, Mark. I can dig a lot deeper with the people who are behind me, but save me the trouble and tell me the truth now and I may be able to help the pair of you."

Mark knew that he was caught. He also knew that it was a waste of time arguing with MI5. They could make a cat talk if need be.

"Look, Stewart, you know as well as I do that Karim was a danger to us all and was best done away with. So Martin and I hatched the plot which did the job. You should be grateful really."

"Maybe, but not only is that bloody murder, Mark, but you've dropped me right in it. You used info that I gave you to carry out a bloody murder. When this comes out, I'll get the sack, thanks to you."

"Do you have to report all this?" asked a shaking Mark.

"'Course I bloody do," Stewart said angrily. "My boss isn't happy because he lost a link in the chain of subversives that took us bloody ages to put together. Look, what I'll do is keep this to myself for a little while. I've been given a new case to look into. Some bloody foreigner was found drowned. I can't promise anything, but you'd better prepare yourself for a load of shit coming your way."

Mark gulped about the news of the foreigner but said, "Okay, Stewart. Look, I'm sorry if I've got you into trouble, and we'd be very grateful for any help."

The pair shook hands and Stewart went on his way. Mark phoned Martin and put him in the picture. They both realised the game was up and wondered what was next.

Chapter 18

James took a call from the face recognition team at Sidcup. "Hello James, we've got a name to that face you sent me a couple of weeks ago."

Oh great, thought James.

"It's a Mark Naylor. His photo was on an army award ceremony, so that was handy."

James asked what degree of certainty they could guarantee. With this new technology, they would give it 95%. *That's good enough for me,* thought James, and took it to Jack's office.

"I've got a name for that photo, sir. They reckon it's 95% accurate. I've even got an address for him. Seems a bit peculiar to be cycling in that town, so far from his home."

"Leave it with me, James. It's a pretty long shot, as there must have been dozens of bikes along that road that day, but stranger things have happened, so I can tell the boss that we're looking into a lead." Jack had a few things to do, and it was a long way out of his area, so it could wait until he was chased from upstairs.

Stewart kept his chat with Mark in wraps for the moment and thought that he'd look into this other business. He called Fred Wade and made an appointment for the following day.

It's good job this other business cropped up. He could tell his boss that he was looking into that rather than the preacher affair.

Fred greeted Stewart next day and got him a coffee. He ran through all the details for Stewart and showed him where it took place on the map on his wall.

He was interested in why MI5 were involved and Stewart gave him the outline that Gustavs was suspected of people smuggling. Fred commented that it wasn't a bad thing that one of that scum had met his end, and Stewart agreed with him.

"Obviously a lot of money in it. A nice address, Ferrari, three or four massage parlours. Not done him any good though, has it?"

Stewart asked if there'd been any developments at this end. "Nope, doesn't appear to be any relevant clues."

"Nothing at all? What was he doing inside the fence at that hour?"

"Well, it seems that Gustavs liked the occasional carp for his dinner and had the habit of poaching one now and again."

"Do we know how often?"

"Well, that red Ferrari is a bit of a giveaway because when we went knocking on doors. Some people had seen it fairly regularly."

"Anything else?"

"Nope, a chap caught sleeping in his car a couple of nights previous."

"Is that near a pub then?"

"No, it's miles away from a pub. Chap said he stopped to make a call and fell asleep. I've got his details if it's worth anything."

"It doesn't seem connected, but I'll take his details please, just in case he happened to see anything relevant." Fred gave Stewart a handwritten name and address and Stewart slipped it into his pocket. They made their goodbyes and promises to keep in touch, and Stewart left.

He got into his car and thought, *What did I do with that bloody piece of paper?* He felt inside his jacket pocket and retrieved it. When he read it, his mouth dropped open.

Oh, for Christ's sake, it couldn't be, could it?

Fred Wade picked up the phone and called Jack West.

"What's new?" he asked.

"No, nothing new, Fred, same shit, different day… You?" laughed Jack.

"Nope, just had a visit from MI5. They're dealing with a case here. A suspected people smuggler got himself killed apparently, bloody good job if you ask me."

"Yeah, similar thing here. Some human piece of shit, raped and murdered a young girl, then got off on a technicality. Someone shot him through the head. It was me who had to tell the parents about their daughter in the first place, not a very pleasant experience, I can tell you. I've managed to keep in touch with them since and had the great pleasure of telling them that they wouldn't have to worry about him anymore. The boss keeps on to me about finding the guilty party, but I can't be bothered really. Tell you what though, we sent a photograph of a suspect on a bike and although it was only a profile shot, with this new technology they've got, they were able to give me a name and address. They're making this job a lot easier for us."

"They won't need us soon, Jack. A local lad, was it?"

"No, miles from here, and ex-soldier, Mark something or other."

"That's funny. That's a name I've just given to MI5. Hang on. It wasn't Mark Naylor, was it?"

"Christ, yes it was. That's too much of a coincidence. Don't do anything until I get back to you."

Fred cut the call and phoned Stewart, who took it as calmly as possible and thanked him.

After placing the phone back in its cradle, he leant back and wondered if he should have Mark arrested but then resisted the idea.

Instead thinking, *This is all too much for me. It's well out of my league. I'll have to pass this up the line.*

Chapter 19

Trying to keep a tremor out of his voice, Stewart called Max Roberts. "Can I pop up and see you sir, please?"

"Yes of course, Stewart. Good news I hope?"

"I'll leave that for your decision, sir."

The meeting didn't last long. Stewart laid out the details as far as he could. Two ordinary people involved in the murder of three criminals. Three vigilante killings, miles apart, no on-site clues, sheer coincidence that the same name had been attached to each investigation.

"What should I do about it, sir?" asked Stewart.

"Nothing yet. I'll want to see those two men, and I'll also want to see the DIs involved."

"All at the same time, sir?"

"Get them here at the same time. I'll decide if I'll want to see them together."

Stewart called Mark first.

"Mark, look, I'm sorry mate, but I couldn't keep all this quiet any longer. I've had to move all the info upstairs and the boss wants to see you—himself. No, you're not being arrested...yet. Just be here on time. In fact I'll send a car round for you both at nine in the morning."

He then called Martin with the same message.

Jack and Fred were next. Both resisted at first, citing previous appointments, which Stewart sidestepped fairly easily. "This isn't a request. It's an order. Be here at 10 a.m. tomorrow."

Chapter 20

Mark drove round to Martin's office. Nervously, he collapsed on to an armchair.

"Now what'll we do?" he asked.

"We've got no option," came the reply. "We'll have to go."

"I don't suppose we'd get very far if we ran away, so yes. Christ! I'm not looking forward to telling Sue about this. We might not be back tomorrow night. Does Julie know anything?"

"Nope, not a thing, but if as you say, we might not come back after tomorrow. I think it's time to let them both know, don't you? Not only are we about to be thrown in jail for the rest of our bloody lives, but I can see two divorces in the not-too-distant future."

"If I know anything about Sue, I doubt if I'll survive telling her. At least that'll get me out of tomorrow."

Martin thought for a moment. "Do you think it'd be an idea to tell them together, or separately at home?"

"Let's do it together! How about a nice meal at the Italian first to make them happy and then maybe a drink at my place and break the news there?" said Martin, who then picked up the phone and booked a table for 7:30.

Both Sue and Julie were delighted to be eating out. They were both fed up with cooking every night, and pleasant company would be nice.

Martin drove to the restaurant without saying a word. "You okay?" asked Julie.

"Yes, of course, just got a lot on my mind at the moment."

"Well, try and pep up before we get there."

Mark and Sue were already at the table when they walked in. Mwah kisses were exchanged, and wine was passed around.

"This is nice," said Julie. "We haven't been out for weeks."

Understandably, the conversation didn't exactly flow, but the two girls kept it going. After about 90 minutes, the bill for £187.48 came and the two men split it with their cards.

As they were finishing their coffees and Italian biscuits, Martin suggested that they finished the evening back at theirs. Sue looked at Mark and nodded approval. A relieved Mark said, "Great."

A few years earlier, Martin had had a nice, modern conservatory built onto the back of the house overlooking their smallish but well-kept garden, a couple of white settees with low tables in front of them provided the minimalistic furniture. Martin opened a bottle of Prosecco and tried to fill up the four glasses carefully in spite of his shaking hand.

"You two going away this year?" asked Sue.

"Actually we've been looking for a place to buy somewhere along the south coast where we can spend weekends," replied Julie. "What about you?"

"We had a nice week in France about a month ago, and I'd like to go again, but maybe a bit further south if we can manage it."

Martin interrupted, "I think that might go on hold for a while, Sue. Mark and I have something to tell you both."

Sue looked at Mark and Julie sat up straight. Martin continued, "Us two," nodding at Mark, "have got to go into London tomorrow morning to answer some questions about a couple of crimes that we're suspected of being involved in."

Julie stared at Martin. "What sort of bloody crimes? As far as I know, we don't have a money problem, so you haven't robbed a bank…or have you?"

"No, it's a bit worse than that. It's a murder enquiry."

"Murder?" shouted Sue, looking straight at Mark. "Whose?"

Mark stuttered, "Do you remember that chap who got off from the rape and murder of the young girl?"

"Yes, horrible sod. Everybody remembers it."

"You'll also remember that I went to the Czech Republic in one of Martin's lorries a few months ago." Sue nodded. "I went to buy a rifle and I was the one who shot the bastard."

The two girls looked at each other in a stunned silence.

"Oh, Mark, how could you just kill someone in cold blood?"

"I'm a soldier, Sue. It was no big deal. In any case we thought that we were doing society a favour."

Julie asked, "So how did they catch you? I haven't read anything in the papers about it?"

"It goes on from there. I didn't get caught. We both thought that it was so easy, so we looked to see if we could do it again."

"I'm not sure I want to hear this," remarked Julie.

"What was your part in all this?" she asked, looking at Martin.

"I did the arranging and the financial side of it."

"That means you're as guilty as Mark."

"Er, yeah, 'fraid so."

"Go on," said Sue, looking at Mark.

"The Muslim preacher who got blown up."

"Oh no, don't tell me that you did that?"

"Um, yes."

"That's it then, two murders, doesn't matter how you look at it, they're murders. How on Earth did you two, supposedly intelligent men, imagine that you'd ever get away with it? What about us? I don't suppose either of you gave us a bloody thought in all this, did you?"

"The whole point, Sue, was that we were doing society a favour because the justice system wasn't working."

"So you took the justice system into your own hands...sod us? What's happening tomorrow?"

"Mark and I have got to go to MI5 and hear about what's going to happen."

"MI5, Christ! How the bloody hell did they get involved? You two won't be coming home tomorrow!" yelled Sue. "Did that chap who came round that night have anything to do with this?"

"Yeah, Stewart works for MI5 now. When he came round, it was because he was suspicious and was making enquiries."

"Is that everything?" asked Julie.

"No, not quite," came from Martin.

"Oh shit! Well, let's have it all now before I pack my bags."

"Come on, Julie. Maybe it won't be too bad."

"Not too bloody bad?" she yelled. "Are you both bloody mad? You two have murdered two people. You're going up to MI5. There's not much worse than that. They'll hang the bloody pair of you. Get me another drink, and make it a strong one."

Shaking like a leaf, Mark continued, "When we were in France Sue, do you remember the chap who asked us to hide him in our car?" Sue nodded, wiping her eyes with her handkerchief.

"Well, that gave us the idea of finding the gang leaders who smuggle immigrants here."

"Go on," said Sue, trembling.

"We found one who was doing it and forcing the women to work in those so-called massage parlours."

"Oh, please don't tell us that the pair of you have been going round to them?"

"No, 'course we haven't, but we did manage to rid society of the leader."

"So three murders now?" came from Julie. "You definitely won't be coming home tomorrow, and anyway, I won't be here if you do. I don't want to be married to a bloody murderer."

Chapter 21

Dorothy Green was always at her desk by 8 a.m., so there was always a cup of coffee waiting for her. It was a big desk, as was only to be expected for the home secretary.

Dorothy had held the post for about 18 months, and despite all her intentions, she had spent most of that time reacting to events rather than being proactive, as she had hoped. She was coping quite well with the day-to-day problems, although she was under constant criticism from the opposition and some newspapers.

Coming from the education department, she was unused to security problems and COBRA meetings, so she leant heavily on advice from both MI5 and MI6. Despite them not always being in agreement, both were very helpful, recognising that she had literally been thrown in the deep end, and expected to make decisions in matters that were completely new to her.

Her diary for today showed that she had a video appointment at 3 p.m. with her French counterpart concerning the fishing quotas, now that Britain had left the EU. This was more a problem for the food and Agriculture ministers, but there seemed to be a difficulty over misinterpretations. How she was supposed to answer that, she didn't quite know, but she'd listen to the problem.

Margaret, her PA, popped her head round the door. "Sorry to butt in, minister, but Col Roberts of MI5 has been on the phone asking for half hour of your time this morning. There are no other appointments this morning, so I gave him 10:30 if that's okay with you?"

"Yes, that's fine, Margaret. Did he give you any details of the purpose of his visit?"

"'Fraid not, minster."

Dorothy had met Col Max Roberts before several times, a pretty down-to-earth man, as were most of the security service people. Very single-minded they were, with very little time for politics, a bit shoot-first-and-ask-questions-later type, so she thought it must be important for him to want to speak to a politician.

At 10:30 on the dot, the intercom announced Col Roberts' arrival, and Dorothy asked for him to be sent in.

Max had been in this office several times, but with other people, so this was first visit alone.

"Come in, colonel. How very nice to see you," said Dorothy, shaking hands with him.

"Please take a seat. What brings you here, and how can I be of assistance?"

Max reminded the HS of the continuing people-smuggling issue and how his department was in constant talks with four other European security departments about catching the rogue gangs who organised the channel crossings.

"I'm sure, minister, that you're aware that the highly secretive combined operation is tightening the net around these gangs and there should be significant arrests in the next three or four months."

"That's good to hear, colonel. It's a source of embarrassment to us and all the EU countries and of course from the media. Do you need any help from me?"

"Yes, ma'am. We do," answered Max.

He then went into detail about the arrests that were due to be made and about how the publicity could damage the current investigations.

"Yes, I can see that, colonel. So what are you suggesting?"

In the next 15 minutes, Max came up with a solution that only the HS could countenance. Dorothy fired a lot of further questions and, after much thought, said that she would only agree if Max could guarantee absolute complete secrecy. She needed to know all the names and backgrounds of those involved and to be kept in touch with all developments.

A relieved Max was happy with that and left the home secretary to deal with the implications and to make the necessary phone calls to some important people. She then looked forward to some lunch and to practising her French, in which she would in no doubt be tested during her later conversation.

Chapter 22

Just before 9 a.m., a black Range Rover, with someone seated next to the driver, who they assumed to be an assistant if things got too heavy, picked up Mark and then Martin five minutes later. Both of whom wore suits and fairly sober ties.

The MI5 headquarters in London is a very large and impressive building overlooking the Thames near Vauxhall Bridge.

The car dropped them at the entrance just before 10. The man inside the door silently pointed to the reception desk and they walked over the highly polished tiled floor to give their names and were told to take a seat.

Ten minutes later, Jack West came in looking around and was told the same. Fred Wade was next. He saw Jack, waved and walked over. "Better sign in first, Fred." Fred walked over to the desk, signed in and then sat next to Jack.

Neither of them knew the two faces sitting close to them, and neither Mark nor Martin knew the two police officers.

When Mark and Martin's names were called, they stood up and were greeted by Stewart.

Fred looked at Jack and shrugged his shoulders in as much to say, "It's those two we're here for."

Looking at the two DIs, Stewart said, "You wait here, gents please. You'll be called shortly."

Stewart led Mark and Martin to a lift that took them quickly up four floors. The doors of the lift opened to a big room divided by glass partitions, some larger than others and some misted over. At the end was a solid wall and they walked through a highly polished door leading into the office of Max Roberts' secretary. A further door led into Col Max Roberts' office. It was an impressive corner room, large, comfortably furnished with an armchair and a leather sofa behind a long glass low-level table. Stewart brought up two chairs and put them in front of the huge desk.

"G'morning, gentlemen," began Max brusquely.

"Do you two know what you've done and how much bloody trouble you've caused?" He continued, "Do you also know the penalties that you're both facing?"

Before they could answer, Max went on, "At least 25 years each, and no remission. You and your families will be ruined. Your names and faces will be spread over every bloody newspaper in the world. And on top of that, you're a complete bloody embarrassment to the police, to me, to MI5 and to the government. Now get out, and wait outside until I call you."

Stewart took them out and sat them on two chairs next to a window overlooking the river.

Martin looked at Mark. "Oh, fuck, I didn't like that. I wish we hadn't started now."

"It's a bit too late for that, Martin. We were only trying to do a bit of good and rid society of those bloody morons who were a risk to everyone."

Their conversation was interrupted by Stewart bringing in the two DIs.

Once in Max's office, they were seated in the chairs vacated by Mark and Martin.

Max began again. He wasn't really looking forward to this particular conversation.

"G'morning, gents. Sorry to bring you both up here, but this has got to be solved before any news gets out. I've spoken to the home secretary, and we've come to the conclusion that a public court case about these murders will do nobody any good, quite the reverse in fact. Those two outside will become martyrs, we'll all look fools and a lot of information will come out that we'd prefer to keep to ourselves. The home secretary will speak to the met chief of police, and you will be told not to continue with your investigations."

Fred turned to look at Jack and back to Max.

"I'm not too happy about that, sir. We've got a duty to bring criminals to justice, and those two should not go unpunished."

"I'm not happy either," continued Max, "but we, and our friends on the continent, are almost ready to catch a whole raft of people smugglers, and if this gets out, a lot of them will disappear, and we can't let that happen, I'm afraid. The whole operation has been going on for about 18 months now and we can't afford for all that work to be jeopardised. Give it some thought and I'm sure you'll agree that this is the best step. Those two outside will be warned of the most dire circumstances if they ever breathe a word of this. So thank you for coming here today. If you're ever asked any searching questions from any quarter, especially from the press, I'm sure you're both capable of dealing with them. Stewart, bring those two back in please."

Fred and Jack reluctantly stood up and shook hands with Max and were taken outside by Stewart, who arranged for them to be shown the way out.

Once Mark and Martin were seated again, Max spoke.

"I've spoken to the home secretary about you two, and reluctantly we've agreed to put the charges against you on hold for a while. If one word gets out, the charges will be implemented immediately. After instructions, the two police officers have also reluctantly agreed not to press charges at this time. You haven't got away with these offences. They'll be hanging over you until the day you die. Before you go, I've got one question. How did you get the information about Abdul Karim?"

A startled Martin answered, "It was all guess work actually. It just happened to come right for us. We'd seen him on TV and read the newspapers. Mark then spent some days watching him and deciding what to do. The opportunity came when my company had to deliver the large pot."

Max seemed satisfied, and Stewart managed to hold in a sigh of relief.

They were then dismissed and they stood up and shook hands with him and said, "Thank you."

Stewart accompanied them to the lift and said, "G'bye."

Our two heroes almost ran out of the building and headed for the nearest pub.

"Time for a holiday, I think! That's if Julie's still there when I get home," said Martin. "We're going as far away as possible, for as long as possible."

"I think we'll join you," said Mark.

"No, you bloody won't. It was great being with you for these last few months or so, Mark, but I'm having a break from you in case we come up with any more crazy ideas."

THE END

Milton Keynes UK
Ingram Content Group UK Ltd.
UKHW020445281123
433366UK00013B/269